HOW TO DRAW AND SAVE YOUR PLANET FROM

ALIEN INVASION !

Sheldon Cohen

Dover Publications, Inc.
Mineola, New York

Bibliographical Note

How to Draw and Save Your Planet from Alien Invasion!, first published by Dover Publications, Inc., in 2011, is a slightly altered republication of the work originally published by Yellow Monkey Publishing, Canada, in 2005. Some corrections have been made to the text, and Practice Pages have been added at the end of the book.

International Standard Book Number

ISBN-13: 978-0-486-47833-3
ISBN-10: 0-486-47833-5

Manufactured in the United States by Courier Corporation
47833501
www.doverpublications.com

HOW TO DRAW AND SAVE YOUR PLANET FROM

ALIEN INVASION !

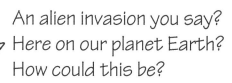

An alien invasion you say?
Here on our planet Earth?
How could this be?

It was bound to happen. The mysterious crop circles, the amazing UFO sightings, and the unbelievable alien encounters! The signs were all there! It was only a matter of time before it happened!

Now it's up to you, your pencil, and imagination to draw and save your planet before the aliens have a chance to take over Earth! Don't spare any paper, don't worry about wasting too much pencil lead, and don't fret about using up your eraser, the world is depending on you to
come to the rescue and save the planet!

BASIC SHAPES

Before we begin let's make sure that you're totally equipped with the right supplies and are prepared to face this invasion!

Pencils on hand? How about an eraser? Do you have plenty of paper? Most importantly don't forget to bring your imagination because this is the most important part!

Okay, let's get to it!

Are you a bit nervous facing this invasion? Take a deep breath, relax and start warming up by drawing a few basic shapes. This will help you become more comfortable with your creations! You know what they say, practice makes perfect!

Let's start off with your home planet.
A nice, cozy, quiet little place.
Not too hot (unless you're living in
a volcano!), not too cold (have you been
to Siberia lately?)

...Earth.

Of course, you'll need to know how to draw the other planets in your solar system as well as the rest of the galaxy, especially if you want those aliens to get to your planet and destroy it, or try to...

START WITH YOUR HOME

P L A N E T S

Every planet doesn't have to be round. Out in the galaxy anything goes beyond your wildest imagination! The planets that you design are strictly up to you!

The universe
is a big place,
so drawing
a map for the
galactic
visitors is a good
idea too, just in
case
they can't find an
inter-galactic gas
station
to ask for
directions!

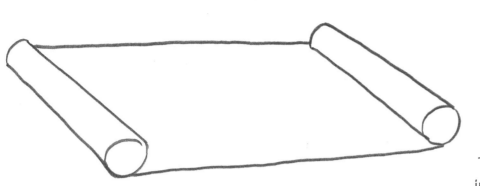

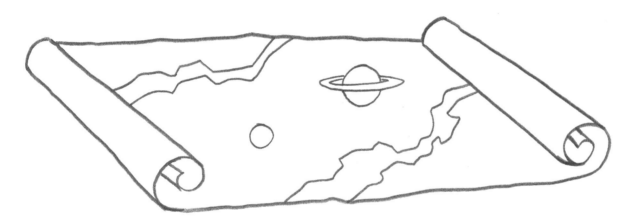

I N T E R · G A L A C T I C   M A P

ARE YOU READY TO DRAW AND SAVE YOUR PLANET FROM

ALIEN INVASION?

YOU
ARE
HERE

A L I E N   S P A C E S H I P S

Aliens will be traveling across the galaxy in their state-of-the-art space crafts. How big will those ships be? Are they as big as an entire city? Are they as small as a green pea? How about somewhere in between? Here are a couple of ideas to help you load up those trekking creatures. (Note: Since traveling light years across the galaxy may take years and years, you may want to draw some alien washrooms in the space crafts!)

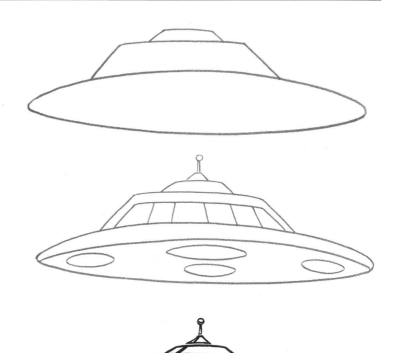

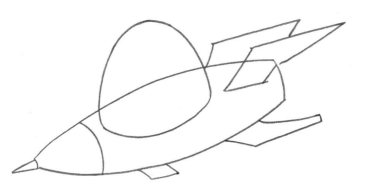

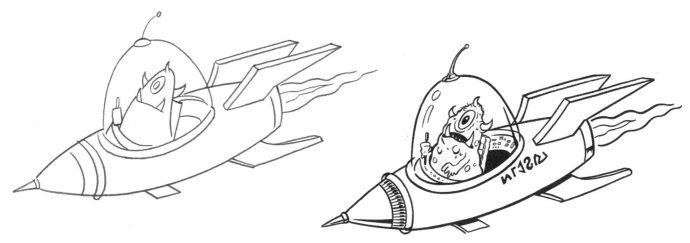

What will the aliens look like? How will they dress?
(Casual I hope -unless it's a black-tie affair.)
Dressing up your visitor:
They say clothes makes the person,
in this case "the alien" !

Alien visitor no. 1
dressed in galactic clothing
"I come in peace"

Alien visitor no. 2 dressed in
Non-galactic clothing
"I come in three-piece suit"

DRESSING UP YOUR VISITOR

WHAT THEY LOOK LIKE

How many eyes will they have? 1? 2? 3? 36? 423? 3,103? 2,333,437? How many arms? How many legs? Will your alien have one head or two? All this doesn't matter. When it comes to drawing aliens, anything goes - there are no rules.

They can be big, small, hairy, scary, fluffy, slimy, friendly, two-eyed, and three-eyed, no one really knows what they really look like, it is strictly up to you, your pencil, and your imagination. Remember, start drawing lightly at first, working with the basic shapes for the aliens.

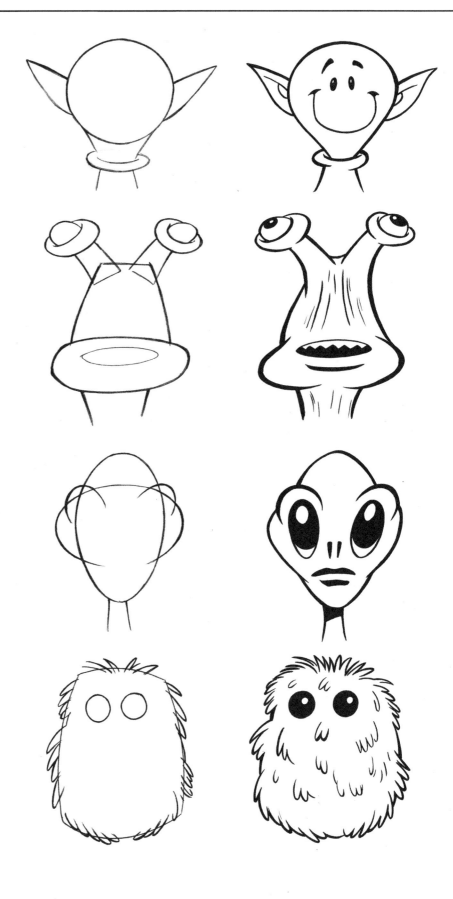

EVEN MORE MONSTERS

Here are a couple of ideas you could work on.

Rock Creature Warrior

This is perfect for those merciless attacks on your planet.

Slimy, Grimy, Smelly Slop Creature

If you plan to battle this dude, make sure your team is equipped with nose plugs.

SMELLY SLOP CREATURE

T
H
E

G
I
A
N
T

B
R
A
I
N

A
L
I
E
N

Giant Brain Alien

This super-powered highly
intelligent cranium beast would make
an excellent guest
on any game show.

Robot Invaders
There is nothing like fighting an
over-sized tin can.

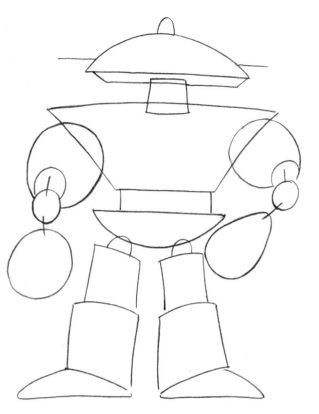

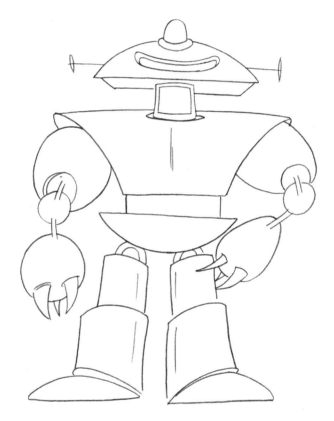

Multi-tentacle Beast

This fella would make a great
hockey goalie!

Multi-eyed Thing
I pity his eye doctor, or his dentist, for that matter!

M
U
L
T
I
-
E
Y
E
D

T
H
I
N
G

Martian Microbe
Yech!

Egg-Hatching Dripazoid
Double yech!

P
L
A
S
M
O

P
L
A
X
Y

A
N
I
M
A
L

Plasmo Plaxy Animal
Isn't he pretty…pretty ugly!

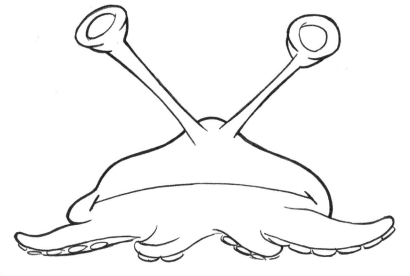

Three-eyed Nebuloid
From Neptune

This fella may be friendly!
Nah…I don't think so!

THREE-EYED NEBULOID

Smelly Cheese-Faced Invader

The important question
–is he a bad cheese
or a GOUDA cheese?

Are you still undecided about what type of alien to create?

How about designing a top secret, government classified alien warehouse, filled with various alien body parts that you can use for your creations.

(Psst... keep this drawing hush-hush! This warehouse is supposed to be strictly classified so draw some guards around your building!)

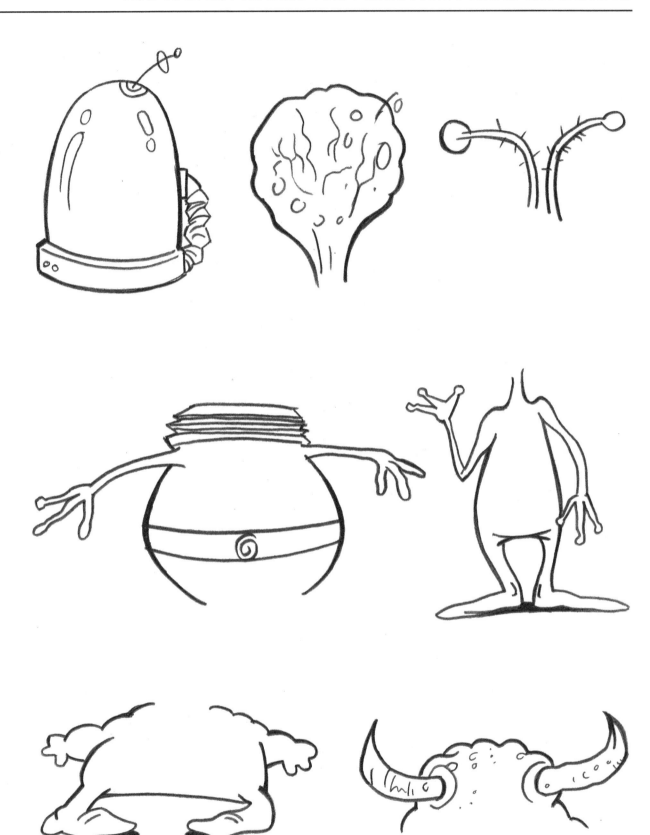

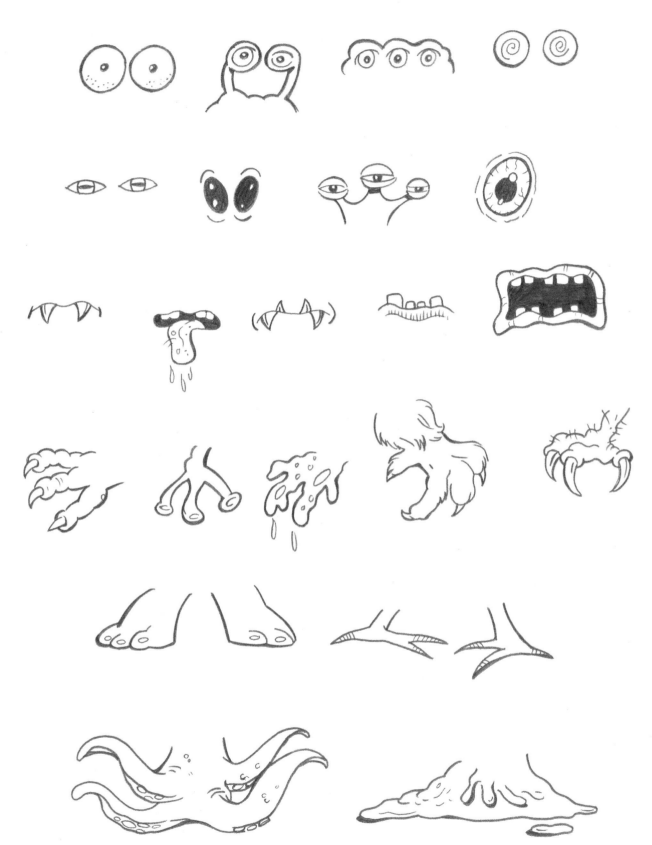

T
O

Y
O
U
R

S
T
A
T
I
O
N
S

They're here!

Battle stations!
    Battle stations!

Red alert!
    Red alert!

Code red!
    Code red!

Danger!
    Danger!

This is not a drill!
This is not a...

okay,
I guess
you've got
the message
already.

Space headquarters has spotted a blip on the radar screen!
Emergency sirens go off everywhere!

There's panic in the streets!

Aliens are landing and attacking!

EARTH IS UNDER ATTACK

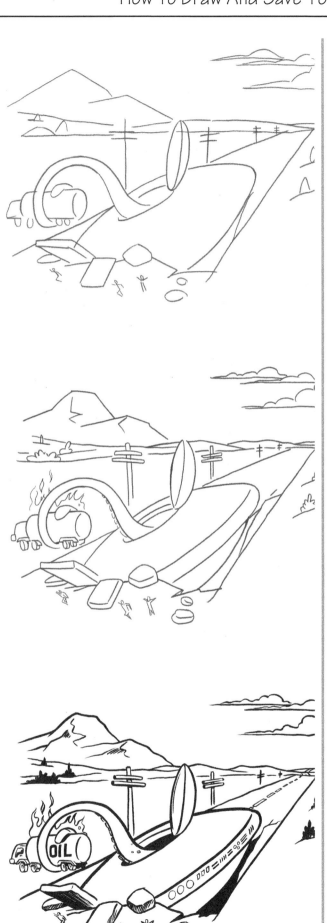

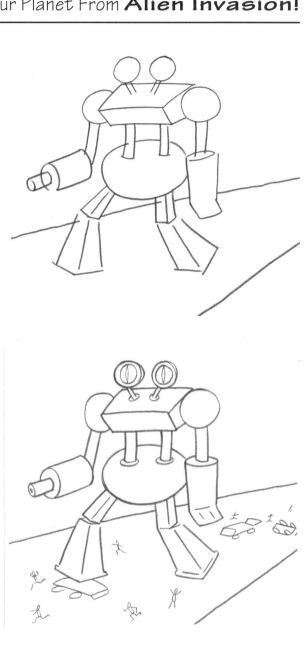

FRIGHTENED EARTHLINGS

How scared will people be? That's up to you.

Worried   Scared a bit   Totally freaked-out!

The news breaks out all over the world! Newspapers, Radio and Television are informing the public with non-stop around the clock news about the alien invasion!

EXTRA EXTRA EXTRA INVASION

TELEVISED COVERAGE

Quick, design a television and let the public know what's going on!
Draw up the President, a news reporter, whoever you would like to deliver the Earth shattering news!

Secret Service
to the rescue!

Who will you draw
to help you battle
this invasion?

The army?
The navy?
The marines?
The police?
The local boy
scouts?

Or maybe
the little old lady
down the street
who swings a
mighty cane?

A
S
K
I
N
G

F
O
R

H
E
L
P
.
.
.

Okay, so an old lady is not going
to do much, but maybe if you equip
her with a super-mega-sub-atomic-
alien-laser-obliterator-blaster…

A
S
K
I
N
G

F
O
R

H
E
L
P
.
.
.

Scouts are always prepared.

The Police will protect you!

Fire fighters are standing by!

The Army is ready for action !

MORE HELP ON THE WAY

CHOOSE YOUR CHARACTERS

Like a movie director you will need to select your main characters, as well as a cast of extras to help you out.
Here are a couple of characters you can choose from:

Construction worker

Soldier

Senior citizen

Teenage boy

Teenage girl

Hysterical lady

Professor

Policeman

Street bum

Average Joe

Taxi driver

Movie Star

Doctor

Street cleaner

Nerd

Tough guy

Really tough guy

CHOOSE YOUR CHARACTERS

Create an amazing muscle-bound superhero who possesses awesome spectacular powers.

Your heroes' faces should be tough-looking!

No, tougher than that.

Tougher…

Perfect!

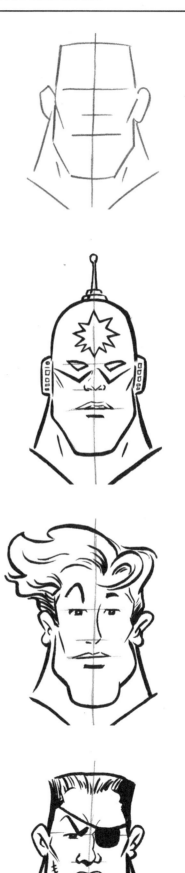

CREATE A PERFECT HERO

Supplies!

Supplies!

You can't prepare a plan of attack without the proper supplies!

You know, useful things like maps, compasses, binoculars, night-vision goggles, walkie-talkies, canteens of water (okay, soda will do…), food, nothing too messy.

You can't battle aliens with chocolate-covered fingers.

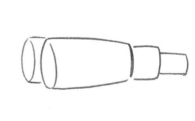

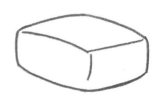

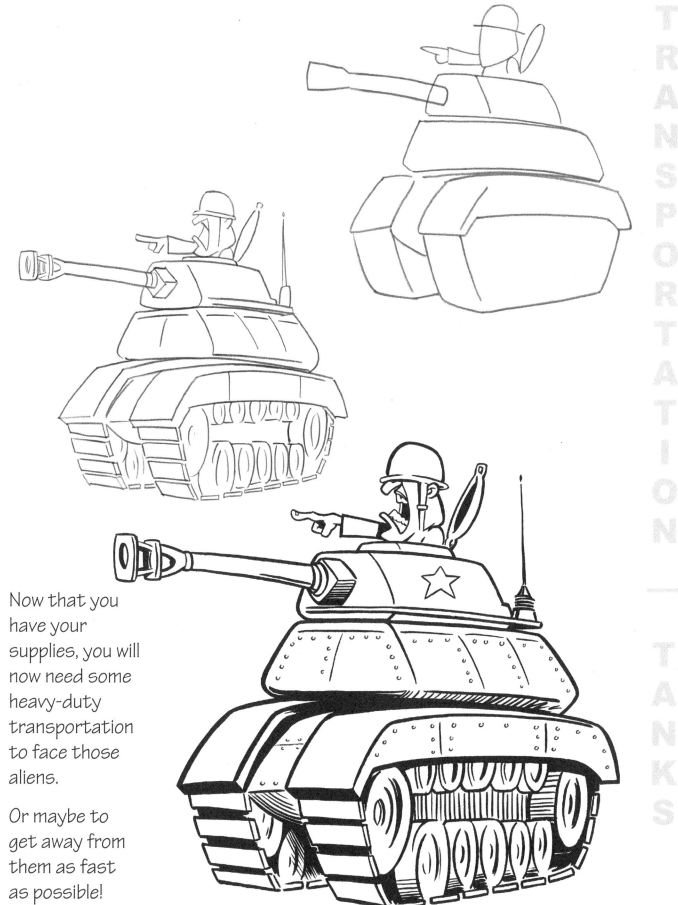

Now that you have your supplies, you will now need some heavy-duty transportation to face those aliens.

Or maybe to get away from them as fast as possible!

FIGHTER JETS

The Eiffel Tower (Paris)

Although those uninvited space beings are coming to conquer your planet, they are still considered to be out-of-town tourists, so you might want to draw some worldly famous places so that they can take the sights while at the same time, invade.

Here are a couple of scenarios that you can use during this moment of chaos.

Ahh!... Paris in the spring is a fine time for an invasion.

"Oh, bonjour monsieur green thing ..."

The Empire State Building (New York)
Just make sure it's ape-free
that weekend!

The Great Pyramids (Egypt)
Wait a minute, haven't they been
there before?

Your Local School
Try not to cry too much!

The local gas station
Maybe they'll need a fill-up for the way back!

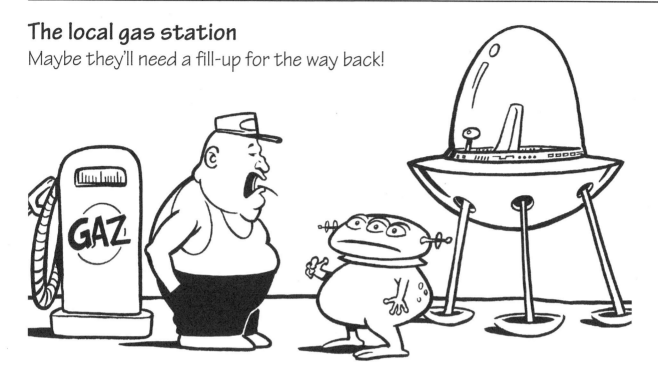

The donut shop
A chocolate donut with a large coffee, please.
By the way, the donut shop may have a fighting chance since
there will probably be lots of
policemen there!

HOW ABOUT A WHOLE CITY

Thanks to you and your creative pencil, the aliens are soon defeated !

GALACTIC SPACE PRISON

They are quickly placed in a special Outer Galactic Space Prison, which you've personally created on the moon (or on Mars, Jupiter… or even Mercury… actually forget Mercury, the summers there are unbearable!).

The President and various world leaders are congratulating you! The mayor presents you with the key to the city, the chief of police, the CIA, FBI, and yes, even your family, who thought you were wasting your time doodling, thank you.

The phone hasn't stopped ringing, everybody wants the story, the news channels, the science channels, the heroes channel and yes, even the food channel (go figure!).

TV cameras, photographers, newspaper journalists, and microphones are everywhere.

CONGRATULATIONS!

COFFEE SHOP

Of course, some aliens you are able to rehabilitate into our society. They soon take on odd jobs and begin leading normal lives. (Well, almost normal!)

Congratulations on a job well done! Because of your awesome cartooning skills and your creative imagination you've managed to save your planet from a possible alien take-over! As well, you have given yourself tons of cartooning tips and ideas which will help you out if those galactic invaders decide to return. Draw your face in the newspaper headline below, you deserve it!